SNOW & CARAMEL

A Post-Apocalyptic Dystopian Thriller

Jay Kerk

Cover design by: Ahmed Moghazy upwork.com/fl/ahmedmoghazy2

Thank you, the reader, for purchasing this book and for investing your time into reading it.

If you like this book, please take the time to rate it and write a short review. Having reviews and ratings for such books are key for their success.

Follow me on social media if you want to know about my upcoming work.

Thanks again and happy reading!

CONTENTS

SPECIAL THANKS

**TO JO LAVENDER AT INKPOT EDITING FOR
HER EDITING AND PROOFREADING SUPPORT.**

CHAPTER 1

The sound of machines crunching and huffing was the first thing I heard as I took the breath and opened my eyes. I was not sure whether I had drawn the breath myself, or the machine had pumped air through the tube in my mouth. The air kept puffing every few seconds.

At the moment, I was glad they had woken me from the frozen hibernation state I had been fixed in moments before. I had a powerful urge to cry. While they had been freezing me, I had felt empty, devastated, and I could sense the remnants of the sorrow at the edge of my mind, like a shadow. I had no idea how much time had passed.

I was lying down, strapped to a metal structure, which only supported my lower back. My buttocks were practically in the air, my shoulder blades stiff and trembling with the effort of holding me up. I could not get the tube out of my mouth; my limbs were attached to metallic extensions protruding from the machine.

"Where is Caramel?" I whispered.

During the freezing process, my chest had ached and I'd

sobbed, begging for one of the staff to tell me where Caramel was. I was terrified that someone had bought her, or that she'd fallen ill, or that they'd discovered she was of no worth to them and killed her.

The technician responsible for my freezing should not have told me, but he did. He said they were also freezing her. His words brought me comfort – slight, but there. Knowing she was alive was good enough, though I had no idea what the future would hold. I knew we might not be unfrozen together, and that the shop owner might keep us frozen for a long time, and that perhaps no customer would buy us. If we were not sold, they would have to cut their losses and end us. Freezing would become equivalent to death unless someone bought us.

Caramel, my thirteen-year-old sister... there was only three years between us, but the thought of her enduring the needles of freezing pain made me sick.

Humanoids, that was what they called us. We were *humans*, just... smaller. We didn't grow over two feet tall, and long ago, my people had moved away from the cities, away from civilization – toward the mercilessness of disease, radiation, and traps set deep in the wilderness. We lived as far as we could from regular-sized humans, and we feared their cruelty and injustice.

Was there a chance that the world had changed while I had been frozen? It might have been eons. Could I dare to hope that justice and rights were again sacred, as they had been in the old time?

Perhaps, but if there was a chance, it was so slim one might miss it by blinking. The chances of the shop even keeping us alive for that long were almost non-existent; freezing was expensive. It had probably only been a few months.

Realistically, I could only hope that a person had purchased us, and not an organization that would dump us in camps and treat us like slaves. I could not imagine my life without my sister, so I shut my eyes and prayed that the buyer would choose us both. Prayers felt infinitesimally small, but I had no other power.

Maybe the buyer was a wealthy and powerful humanoid, and on a mission to free captured humanoids.

The machine made a squeal; the support under my back started rotating, and within seconds, I was erect. The attachments binding my limbs moved, and I moved with them as if I was sprinting. It shocked my stiffened muscles and hurt enough to bring tears to my eyes. The machine paused, and I sighed in relief – and then suddenly, five needles pricked me in the back in a single jab of concentrated pain, and I was running again. I tried to scream, but I couldn't.

Other than the machine, the room was empty, but when I managed to focus ahead of me, I saw a window of black glass, and I could make out the movement of humans behind it. I guessed that the technician, the buyer, and probably the shop owner stood behind the glass.

To distract myself from the burn of my arms, still forced by the machine that held me, I closed my eyes and recalled my father's stories about the early days of the humanoid. From what I had memorized, I knew that the earth had rebelled against the humans.

Changes started with the warming weather drying up the lands, followed by harmful radiation rays that took the lives of many creatures and changed the lives of the rest. When resources decreased, nations fought with toxic weapons, further damaging the earth. We knew the Nation Wars as the two-decade nuclear wars.

In the year 2054, scientists had revealed humanoids to the world, and they had confirmed that we originated from human beings. Radiation had caused a change in our genetics, keeping us small, and we tended to be hairier all over our bodies, but other than that, we were identical to humans.

The vast majority of humans didn't believe them. They called us abominations, mutations, mistakes born of animals, and not human beings. Human bounty hunters tracked us and treated us like dogs.

Before they captured Caramel and I, we had lived in the Rocky Mountains of New Mexico, and the year was 2235. Our village had been in one of the many habitable areas on the continent, but was probably among the least livable. We always faced difficulties with finding food, but we thought we were safe from the humans. As humanoids, we could live nowhere else. Humans wanted to capture us to use us for heavy labor and risky missions in radioactive zones.

I remember when they attacked our caves; they crowded the children into the vehicles and gathered the adults in the cave. While waiting in the trucks, pressed among other crying children, I had heard the gunshots. I had gripped the bars and closed my eyes, because there was nothing – nothing – that I wanted to see.

How long had we been frozen? A month? A year? Twenty years?

I didn't care if a thousand years had passed. I just cared about Caramel, and whether I would ever see her again. The only person left for me in the world was my sister.

The machine calmed down, and the extensions relaxed their grip on my limbs. My breath caught, and I felt tears on my face, though I hadn't known I was crying. The machine moved me into a sitting position, manipulating my arms and legs in a mockery of human movement. A moment later, I was released.

A human entered the room. He was over five and a half feet tall, a normal-looking human. To me, he seemed a giant.

"Where is my sister? I beg you, mister; can you please tell me? Please?"

He took me by the neck and moved my head into a muzzle and tightened it. His hands were rough. He produced an old piece of cloth with a fabric belt tied at the waist and dressed me briskly, tugging it into place. All I could do with the muzzle was hum and avoid thinking about how thin I had become.

I jerked my chin and tried to get some words out, longing to tell him that the cloth stank enough to make me retch. He smacked me in the back of the head, then pressed down on my head to make me kneel. Stiff and sick with terror, I did.

He left the room for a few minutes and came back with a metal cage. "Inside."

He mounted the box on a trolley, and we started moving. I had to balance by sticking my head to the corner and clinging to the bars, catching glimmers of the world through tightly woven metal.

After some lifting and grunting, the door of the cage opened to the rear interior of a vehicle. I caught a glimpse of the car as the cage was maneuvered in. It was an 8-wheeler, an all-terrain model. Elders from the village had told us that the car was so reliable it could withstand an explosion.

I stood up as the rear door slammed shut, and the lock clicked.

CHAPTER 2

The vehicle's enormous interior could have fitted eight humans in the back and three up front, including the driver. About twenty humanoids would have fitted in the back; the seats had been stripped out, leaving just empty, unwelcoming space.

I went to a window and stretched up on my toes, my hands grasping high above my head – but I could not reach the window's frame. If I could have lifted myself up, I would have seen the market.

I recalled when the bounty hunters had first dropped us here. Flooding water had covered most of the asphalt, and the entire market had reeked of fish. Neon signs had lined the street, identifying the shops – but I hadn't had time to read them. Reading was not a strength for any humanoid. We did not have schools and books like humans; we had to rely on what the elders and adults wrote – just scratches on bark and slate, shaky and difficult to read. We rarely had time for it anyway, between hunting and surviving.

My name was Snow, and I knew what Snow meant. Father had told us that hundreds of years ago, snow fell at high altitudes like the mountain we lived on. He said our Rocky Mountains hadn't seen snow for thousands of years. Snow was like rain, but rain turned to brittle, biting ice in the freezing clouds. Snow was what happened when the world was cold, and water became strong and powerful.

Why wasn't it called white ice? I didn't know. Father and Mother named me Snow because my skin and hair were white – not so uncommon for humanoids as for humans. I had red eyes too. Albino was the term the humans used.

Mother and Father had also named Caramel for her looks. A light brown stickiness formed by heating a sweetener called sugar – apparently similar to honey. Once burned, the product became tastier, and the humans called it caramel. Ironically, sugar was white before the heating. We never saw sugar, but the elders had said sugar resembled the desert sand – just paler and prettier.

Tears filled my eyes, and I realized all that Mother and Father had left behind were beautiful memories – and those, only in my mind and my sister's. There was nothing more of them, nothing at all. The bounty hunters had surely killed them.

I wondered what my fate would be. Freezing was a business, and for them to make a profit, they had to feed us little and sell us quickly – another reason to believe we had probably not been frozen for that long. To make the deal better, they often kept siblings together and offered them at a discount. I hardly dared to hope that meant Caramel might join me – but the man had gone somewhere, and we hadn't left yet, so maybe, maybe, maybe...

The rear door slammed open, and two men placed the same metallic box on the edge of the car. Caramel was crying and flailing, and I heard her before I saw her. One man in an orange overall opened the door of the box, and Caramel stumbled out.

I grabbed her and turned her toward me and threw my arms around her. She felt tiny in my grip, and I had to grit my teeth to resist the urge to hug her too hard. She reached up and unfastened the muzzle, freeing my face so we could talk. She threw it aside in disgust, and I pulled her back into a hug.

"I missed you a lot," I whispered.

"Me too, a lot."

I felt her tears on my shoulder.

She had not changed much, though she had lost a lot of weight. Her shiny brown hair had grown long to her shoulders and covered her back and what I could see of her torso under the rags we had been bundled into. My own hair had grown long too; my chest and shoulders were heavy with it.

Loud snickering coming from the left side of the vehicle made us pause. The front door opened; another human took the driver' seat. He was bigger than the first two men and dressed differently, wearing something that looked like armor. He sighed as he closed the door and took off his radiation-absorbing helmet and radiation-reflecting shoulder protectors.

He turned to look at us, pressing his face on the metallic mesh which separated the front seats from the back. He looked rough, a heavy scar marring his face. Caramel shrank back into me, covering her mouth with one hand.

"Gosh. You are furrier than I thought while looking at you in the tanks." He snickered. "I sure hope they didn't trick me. Now speak up; tell me you are not a modified monkey with a chopped-off tail."

I had heard of that – selling humanoids was a lucrative business, and some scammers sold altered monkeys as humanoids.

"Mister." I cleared my throat and felt Caramel's grip on my hand grow stronger. "This is hair and not fur, and we are humans. Bounty hunters captured us in the Rocky Mountains and sold us unfairly on this market."

"Shut up, humanoid. I know what you are," he said, and turned back, starting the ignition while mumbling something we could not hear. It roared, and the car floor began to tremble beneath us.

He hit the accelerator hard and I staggered backwards, tripping over myself and Caramel – we both crashed to the floor. I hadn't even managed to get my feet back before he turned sharply and sent me rolling into Caramel again. I grabbed onto the box and opened my mouth to shout over the engine. Caramel snatched my hand and shook her head.

I frowned. "But if he's reasonable, maybe he'll release us. If we speak more to him, he'll know we're also intelligent creatures. Maybe he has a soft heart. Maybe we can get through to him." I had to shout to her over the roar of the engine.

The car began to shake more violently.

"What's happening?" Caramel gripped onto me.

"I don't know. Climb on my shoulders and look outside."

"What for?"

"Just do it; see if you can see where we are. Maybe when he stops and lets us out of the car, we can escape. Or maybe you'll see the Rocky Mountains, and we can try to figure out how we get back home."

"No, Snow, we can't, and we won't do that. Escape where? The great endless desert or the radiation concentrations? I'll look outside but – but stop talking nonsense. Hold my feet and don't drop me." She swallowed hard and stumbled over to the window.

I followed and grabbed her, lifting her up as high as I could so her feet could rest on my shoulders. She leaned on the frame and we teetered with the swaying of the car, precariously balanced for precious seconds.

"What do you see? Hurry, my shoulders are hurting."

"Everything is orange. It looks like a sandstorm; I can't see anything. There are big rocks on the sides of the road, but nothing else is visible."

I lifted her down and put my arm around her, swaying with the motion of the car. With my other hand, I turned her face and looked down into her big brown eyes. They had not changed – they were still wells of beauty and softness and honey. I would do anything to keep them that way.

"I will not let anything happen to you."

Her eyes filled with tears, and she rested her head on my shoulder. I sat with her for a few minutes, then gestured for her to stay put by the box, and started across the huge car. Twice more, I found myself staggering with the motion of the vehicle, but I crawled until I reached the front.

I was next to the mesh and used my fingers to hook myself to it. I stared at the driver for a few seconds, willing myself to speak.

"Mister? Thank you for purchasing us; we know that we were as good as dead without your intervention. We are forever in your debt. But please, mister, we belong to a good family and have been raised well. Please set us free."

"Get back and sit down." This close, his deep and hoarse voice scared me, but I had to keep trying.

"I beg you," I said. He threw a quick stare at me.

"Where are you taking us? Are you going to hurt us?" I paused for a second, heart beating hard, and tried flattery. "Surely a gentleman like yourself will not."

He was silent. I waited, counting the seconds by my heartbeat and trying not to choke on my own breath.

"What – what year is it? Has it been a generous year for the crops?" I asked.

"Two thousand two hundred and thirty-eight. Same as before. They say maybe in fifty years we might grow a few of the old edible plants."

"Where are you taking us?" I tried.

He flipped open a hatch in the grille and crooked a finger,

signaling me closer. I crept forward a few inches, thinking he wanted to say something without Caramel hearing. He signaled again, and I moved still closer, putting my face against the opening. He was so huge. I could see stubble around his pallid chin, could almost count his coarse eyelashes.

I hardly saw his hand go up, but I felt it come down, felt his gigantic knuckles crash against my cheek while his eyes stayed trained on the road. I staggered, thrown off balance by the blow and the shock, and then I stumbled back away from him. I lost my footing, but scrabbled further backwards, grabbing Caramel and shrinking down against the rear door with her clasped in my arms.

CHAPTER 3

N ight had fallen by the time he stopped the vehicle, and we could not see where we were. He stepped out of the car without saying a word to us. I clutched Caramel, thinking of the horror stories I'd heard about how humans treated humanoids, whether at homes, factories, or camps. Father had never liked to talk about it, but sometimes morbid moods took us, and we pressed him. He'd told us humanoids might be hunted in survival games, or put to work in hazardous places.

The real horror stories came from the mouths of children whose parents were scouts and security men among our people. They said they heard their parents speak about dedicated markets for humanoid flesh, for humanoid slaves, sexual parlors, and hunting games. Once, a story had circulated about humans torturing humanoids for pleasure. The village had been quiet for days after that.

We heard the man's footsteps and the squeaking of a door, and we knew he was back.

"Let's run. I'll bite his hand, you jump down, and we'll run," I whispered.

"Please don't." Her eyes glimmered with tears and she was biting at her lip. "If you make the man angry, he might kill you. And if we succeed in escaping, we won't know where we are. Then radiation will kill us." She sniffed and wiped at her face. "Please don't do anything stupid. At least we have each other. That's enough for now."

I swallowed hard and tried to keep my voice steady. "Okay, okay. Stop crying. It's okay."

Click-clock. He opened the rear door a couple of inches and stretched his hand inside. We both stared at the hand, so big and alien and strong. So demanding. I could have bitten him if I'd wanted to, but I doubted my teeth could really inflict much pain on his huge, muscular arm.

"Come closer. Turn around and stick your head in my hand. Come on now, it's getting late, and I don't want you to loiter in the vehicle." His voice was still gruff.

Caramel looked at me and moved toward the hand. She rested her head on his palm and squeezed her eyes shut tight.

His fingers closed around the hair on the back of her neck and he lifted her, getting a squeak. It didn't hurt much to be lifted by the hair there, but the indignity of it! A second later, the door slammed and my sister was out of my sight again. I stood in silence, able to feel myself shaking, able to feel the blood thudding and my heart bumping and my breath skipping. It was very dark.

A few minutes later, the door opened again, and I was also ordered over. He grabbed me as he had Caramel, and I gritted my teeth as I felt my feet leave the floor, leaving me dangling helplessly in space.

He opened a couple of gates, walked past the front door of the building – huge, from what I could make out in the dark – and walked around the right-hand side of the house, through a third gate. I glanced down at my feet, dangling uselessly below me, and tried not to panic at how helpless I felt. He opened a door and stepped into a long, dark hall.

At the far end, there was another door – behind it, a dim lamp and Caramel, watching the door with alert, frightened eyes. She relaxed fractionally when she saw me, and he put me down beside her. He left, shutting the door, and I grabbed Caramel's hands.

"At least we don't have to worry about the radiation rays in the morning; we have a shelter," she said.

"What if he bought us fancying a humanoid meal?" I asked and immediately regretted it. She became silent and drew away from me.

The door opened again, making us both jump. The man was holding a large hose and told us to come out and strip our clothes off. Not much in the way of clothes anyway – just rags the technician had covered us with.

The water was so cold it hurt. Icy night had long since robbed the day of any warmth the sun had left. I bit my lip and braved it, getting water up my nose as I turned the wrong way against the spray. I choked and snorted, shivering. The spray went off for a moment and he grabbed a bottle, then held it out. "Shampoo."

I had heard of it. It was sticky and heavy and smelled strong, but I poured some on myself and on Caramel, and we scrubbed it through our hair and over our bodies. It wasn't pleasant, but it felt better than the dirt.

The shock of the water started up again, and I almost lost my balance. Caramel shrank behind me, and I did what I could to shield her while letting the water rinse her off. When the jet stopped again, I shook my hair out of my eyes and looked up at the single towel being offered. He was not holding a second.

"Be quick."

I let Caramel start ahead of me to make more use of the towel while it was dry. It didn't do much to get the water out of my long hair and off my body, but it was something. I handed the towel back to him and he gestured us back into the hall and inside the little gloomy room. A bowl of grass had been set on the floor there.

"Mister… What about our clothes? Can you give us something to cover our bodies?" I asked.

"Not needed. Enough hair covers your body; you don't need clothes." He shrugged.

"But this is indecent, and we will get dirty." I gave him the fiercest look I dared. I was determined to show him we were dignified, not animals. "Surely you can spare some –"

His hand snapped out and struck me hard across the lower jaw. I staggered back a step, shocked.

"From now on, you will call me Master, and I'd prefer you not to talk to me unless you're told to." He narrowed his eyes and slammed the door.

Caramel tugged my sleeve gently, eyes round with concern. "Snow, I saw some clothes hanging outside; they weren't as big as human clothes. They must have or have had humanoids, right? Did you see the clothes?"

I shook her off and rubbed my face. "They weren't human-oid clothes. They must be for human children – bigger than us." I paused, thinking. "But perhaps that might be our way out. Their children aren't known for being smart – certainly not as smart as we are. We might be able to trick them into helping us."

Caramel sat down and picked up the bowl, dividing the food in half and setting it between us. I sat by her and watched her eat, wondering what tomorrow would bring.

"You're not eating…"

"I'll eat in a second." She was smaller and slighter than me, and I knew she had to be hungry. Grass was far from a filling meal. I wanted her to eat as much as she needed before I took any; at least then she would sleep.

I was still very damp, so I got up and began to pace to try and dry myself a little. I had made the floor wet, but there wasn't much to be done about that; we would just have to put up with it, as there was nowhere else to sleep. I looked up at the lamp, wishing there was some way I could reach it to turn it off – I had always preferred sleeping in the dark.

"Snow… I'm cold." Caramel lay down with her arms beneath her head to serve as a pillow. I went over and lay next to her.

"I'm a little damp, but cuddle up to me, and we'll soon be warm." I turned to face the wall so she could cuddle against my back. I lay, focusing on her small arms resting against my side, and thought about everything that had led to this.

There had been a time when every human respected humans and humanoids alike; back then, no one called us humanoids. We had been referred to as patients, although we were not sick.

Father had told us that people then obeyed and feared the law, and that anyone who broke it faced punishments in accordance with their actions. He'd told us that you could be punished just for insulting another person, or for discriminating against them; you could lose your freedom or have to pay them coins. There had been something called the police, similar to our marshals, who enforced the rules.

However, the radiation rays and radiation wars tore down the structures of society, and left people starving. They had no choice – they would take work if it meant food and shelter, even without coins. They would sell themselves into years of service for the promise of life.

Eventually, the Leaders allowed purchase by law: any human or humanoid could buy another human or humanoid. The law stated that work must be done in exchange for food or shelter; purchases were not for hunting games or target practice – but I knew those things happened often these days.

In theory, the laws left humans and humanoids equal, yet in our part of the world, only humans bought humanoids, with as little thought and care as if we were plants, or useful rocks. In other places, Father said, humans were also sold that way.

CHAPTER 4

All was quiet for some time in the morning. We could hear voices and movement in the nearby rooms and see daylight coming under the door as one thin ray. We waited impatiently, huddled together, until the man came.

"Come."

I put my arm around Caramel, and we stepped out together.

He led us through the hall and out to the back of the house, where there was a small area that looked much like the deserts I was familiar with – only considerably smaller. There was an enormous wall, with green plants growing up along the borders of it. The wall brought shade to the space, and it looked somehow soft and pleasant.

"This is our home, and this is our garden where we play with our children. We'll feed you every day, as long as you do your work. If you don't work or finish your tasks as I instruct you, I will not feed you; this is our agreement. You'll have a number of duties, but the most important ones are up on the wall. Every day, I will give you the materials and the equipment, and you will go up onto the wall to clean the lenses, and adjust them if you're told to. They collect the radiation rays and throw them back outside."

We both squinted at the wall standing over three or four hundred yards away. It was about fifteen feet high, with stairs at the sides. They led up to a level section which was made up of black rubber and riddled with spikes. Each spike had a big lens attached to its edge, pointing toward the section's floor. I guessed there were over a hundred lenses across the three sides of the wall.

"Carry the bismuth rods to the wall where the spikes are. The area where you will stand is rubber, and I have inserted bismuth rods deep inside the rubber. We have to replace the bismuth every few days because they melt when absorbing the radiation.

"First, look for the mark with red paint. Then check with the steel rods whether the bismuth rods have melted – to do that, hammer the steel one down to its halfway point. If the steel rod doesn't get obstructed by a bismuth one, it's melted and needs replacing. Take the steel one out and nail a fresh bismuth one down in the same place."

We looked at each other.

"Don't get any funny ideas about climbing the top of the wall. You will die if you try to climb it. The top edge is electrified." He paused and grinned. "To prevent big beasts from entering and little beasts from leaving. There's also broken glass laced with poison up there, so I wouldn't recommend risking a cut."

I thought the job was manageable, but he continued. "Adjustments to the lenses have to be done at midday so we know if we've got the angle right. The rods can be changed when the sun is setting, unless I tell you otherwise."

I felt my stomach drop and looked up at him. "But... Master, the midday rays are too strong." I paused, then made myself say it. "The radiation will kill us in months."

"Then what do you propose? Do you want to stay in my chambers while I do the labor? What do you think, little monkey?" He grimaced. "Pfft. Idiot."

I looked down at the floor, feeling giddy. We were powerless. We would die here – either through slow radiation poisoning, or possibly at his hands if we refused.

"Okay. We'll do as you want," Caramel said. Her voice was steady, but I could feel her trembling beside me.

"We will be dead in a year," I mumbled, and the smack to the back of my head informed me he had heard.

He lifted Caramel off the floor, put his face close to her and sniffed, then put her back on her feet.

"Come, I want you to play with the boys."

"Master, what about me?" I asked.

"Start taking the bismuth rods across the yard." He pointed. "Every day we might need to change ten or twenty. The steel rods are larger than the bismuth ones, so remember not to hammer more than a third or half into the hole. Off you go."

Each rod weighed about thirty pounds, and I struggled to carry half my weight across hundreds of yards. It took me two hours to move the pile he had indicated from one side of the small desert to the other, and the sun burned down upon me whenever I entered the parts of the yard the wall didn't shade.

As I was putting down the last rod, I caught sight of Caramel coming out of the house, her hands covering her privates. I dropped the rod and ran to her, my feet slipping in the sand.

"Are you okay? What happened?"

"Nothing, nevermind it," she said. "The house is enormous, and they have two human helpers – at least, that I saw. He also has two children, both boys."

"Did they do anything to you? Did they..." I struggled for a second, trying to find the words. "...touch you?"

"No. I mean, they did, but not as you think. The boys are young and don't understand. The Master said one is seven and the other is ten. They are so tall, though..." She paused. "Almost double our size. They giggled a lot, but they seemed shy. The Master tried to encourage them to play. He started chasing me, and I ran from one room to another, hiding behind things and going under the tables."

"What else?" I stared at her, worried.

"I frightened the boys a bit. I think they find me... strange. They..." She paused again. "I think they think of us... like pets. They started to touch my hair and back. They meant nothing by it, but I was..." She turned away. "I was... embarrassed."

Anger filled my heart as I reached to hug her. Why did some people get to treat other people as toys? What gave them the right? My sister – a pet, to be handled and prodded and pawed over by children who knew no better and cared nothing for her comfort.

We had to leave this place as soon as we could. Death, no matter its form, was better than suffering and humiliation.

CHAPTER 5

Why did some humans act inhumanely? Many answers came to my mind as I lay waiting for sleep that night; cruelty, greed, lack of empathy. However, it occurred to me that the question was wrong. The question I should ask instead was – what makes us human? For each of us, human and humanoid, it was the understanding which led to compassion that made us human. Without it, we were nothing more than intelligent beasts.

Throughout history, at least as far as my limited understanding went, much of the world seem to have been run by beasts in the shape of humans – even in ages we now looked back upon as golden.

Over the next few days, I made a point of scanning the perimeter of the house, and I concluded that we could plan no escape except through the gates at the front of the house.

The room where he locked us at night had a door that opened to the outer part of the house and led to the little desert, and a second door which led to the main house and through which they brought us food. We were not fed in the mornings. The man said it made us lazy, and hunger should serve as motivation for working harder.

I sat one morning, watching that second door and wondering whether he might forget to lock it at some point. If he did, I could slip into the house once the family were asleep, and search for the gate keys.

Caramel was stirring. She propped herself up on her left hand, and with the other hand she began scooping water from our drinking bowl to wash her face. I heard her sniff, and looked over sharply.

"Are you crying? Don't cry, baby girl," I said. "What is it?"

"Something silly, but I miss home." She sniffed again. "I want a toothbrush. And when I'm sad, I just – I just can't help thinking about Mom and Dad. Do you really think they are dead? Is there no chance they're alive?" She looked at me, her brown eyes steady wells of sorrow that broke my heart.

I shrugged and shook my head. I couldn't answer, and she knew anyway.

Humanoids rarely lived to see their fortieth birthday, and our parents were in their mid-thirties. Of what use could they be to any evil entity, especially bounty hunters? They were dead in the cave, probably left to rot in pools of blood, like the other elders in our tribe. Not even buried. It made my heart hard and cold to think of it.

"Please ask him for a toothbrush for me?" she said, and I nodded.

Truc-tick. The external door opened, and the man looked in to give us our orders.

We made significant progress until noon, but Caramel was

dispirited and miserable, prone to tears that tore me apart. I kept encouraging her, promising that soon we would leave this cruel place.

As the afternoon wore on, I grew more and more worried. Caramel did not do well in the heat. The elders in our village had believed that perhaps she had a parasite or something within her, something that left her weaker than she might otherwise have been. If she fell into a fever, I had no idea what the man would do with her.

Around three, the man hollered at us, asking me to come, so I ran. He grabbed me up by the hair on my back and wrinkled his nose in disgust. "Ugh, motherfucker, you stink."

"Working in the sun all –" His fist cut off my words and I tasted blood, hot iron where I had bitten my tongue. My ears rang for a few seconds and when he dumped me back on the floor, I nearly lost my balance.

He rinsed me with the hose, and this time turned an air blower on me. I was dry in minutes, but uncomfortably hot afterwards.

"Behave yourself now. And be friendly." He strode toward the house, and I followed. It was cool inside, and he led me past several open doors, including a dining room and a kitchen, to a comfortable room full of sofas and plush seats, where the two boys and their mother were sitting.

They eyed me, and I stared back at them. I had not yet met any of them. They seemed wary of the presence of a humanoid – no, not a humanoid. We were small humans. We deserved no lesser name.

"Tell him to speak," said the mother.

"Speak." The man waved his hands around, as if he was casting a magical spell.

"My name is Snow, and I am a human, a smaller one. Thank you for having–"

"Oh, shut up before I crack your head open," he spat.

"Daddy, is his skin as white as his hair?" the smaller child asked.

"Yes. Come check it out," he said, and with a swift movement and a dizzying blur, I found myself flying on his knees with my belly down. I tried not to panic, able to feel him moving the hair on my back.

"See, white skin."

"His red eyes are scary." I was fairly sure that was the older boy.

"No, not scary. You should never be afraid of a humanoid. With one punch, you could split him in half." He chuckled. "Understood, boys?"

Out of the corner of my eye, I saw them nodding.

"Now, we played catch with the other one. Let's see how fast this one can run." He grabbed me, and I found myself on my feet again, giddy from the sudden movement.

"See which of us can grab him first. Humanoid, hide below that table, and see how long you can dodge us for."

I folded my arms and didn't move. He shook me hard, and the older boy approached.

"Didn't you hear him?"

I said nothing. Servant, maybe, but I was not going to be

made a plaything.

The boy grabbed my hair and yanked, and I had to bite back a yell. The man shook me again and then joined his son in yanking at my hair. I could feel my eyes watering with pain. I did the only thing I could think of – I snatched the man's hand from my head, turning his shock to my advantage, and sank my teeth into his skin.

His yell was loud enough to deafen me, and then he had me off my feet again, this time holding me by the hair on my head. I screamed, and he hauled me through the house. I saw blurs of the corridor, of fine furniture, and then felt the blinding heat of the little desert outside as he threw me.

"I will deal with you later," he snarled. "You are lucky that I understand that discipline has to be acquired, and you shall acquire it."

CHAPTER 6

My stomach churned, and the acidity burned my throat, so I kept drinking as much water as I could to try and soothe it. The monster was not letting me eat. Caramel had tried to sneak some weeds out to me, but she'd been seen, and it was hardly her fault. Without clothes, she couldn't hide the food anywhere except her hands. As far as I knew, she hadn't been punished for it, so that was something.

To distract myself from my stomach, I sat and thought about the nature of the man that held us. Was cruelty a part of who he was, or had he been taught it as he was teaching his sons? Were all humans fundamentally cruel beneath the surface?

Father had told us that the first signs of cruelty had appeared a long time before the wars, some three or four centuries ago. Humans had transitioned from barbarism to civilization, and then to cruelty. He'd said that back then, people had started packing millions of cattle and birds into tiny spaces to produce edibles like milk and eggs.

Food was not scarce, but greed controlled the decisions that humans made during that time. Father said that a human can no longer be a human if he does not recognize suffering – and I felt that made me more human than our captors had ever been.

Caramel was resting in the room. We had been hammering the rods for hours, taking it in turns to rest and breathe between blows. Now, the man had locked me out of the room, providing me with a chance to study the residence and turn my thoughts to escape.

The whole area was sandy, with patchy rocks here and there. Two types of plants existed in this harsh environment: the low rise green bush and the pointed cactus. They were arranged symmetrically, making a line that lapped along the edge of the wall. Unfortunately for me, I had found no wood from which I could fashion a weapon. Even the rocks were either too small or too big; most would not damage the man, and I couldn't lift those that would.

The hammer weighed as much as the rods, and there was no way I could swing the hammer or the rods to damage the man. Added to that, I would need to be swift to overcome him, especially if his wife or either of the human helpers were nearby. My only other option was to create some sort of sling, like ones we'd used while hunting in the Rocky Mountains. I remembered Father teaching me how to use one, and wondered what he would think of my plans.

If the children of our tribe asked about killing, Father always answered right to the point. He loved the theatrics of teaching, and would shake his head vehemently, eyes closed with a solemness that matched winter storms. "Killing is not okay, especially if the opponent is weaker than you."

The kids – though not surprised by the answer – would

gasp, enjoying the theatrics of the lessons as much as he did.

"Why? Why?" they would chant, and he would look at them gravely. "Because it will stay with you all your life." Then the children would "Ohhhh" with delight.

I remembered it so clearly. The children he spoke to were too young to really understand the lesson, but Caramel and I had understood, and had listened to them puzzle for hours over how to deal with not killing someone who is a threat to you. They had reached the conclusion that I had reached: if you have no other solution, you must kill. I put aside Father and his graveness; he would not have wanted this life for Caramel and I.

A locked gate separated the little desert from the front of the house. Peering through, I could study the front porch – the only outdoor space in which a flowering plant grew. Beyond it, another two gates we would have to pass through.

With the gate I was leaning on, that meant we needed to overcome three hurdles to escape through the front. However, when I stared at the front gates, I grew increasingly sure that if we could make it that far, we might be able to slip through the bars. They were wider than the garden gate, and Caramel and I were both thin.

The bases of all three gates had bars piercing down into the sand. My gate did not budge when I shook the bars; it must have been bolted to the ground. I could dig a tunnel under the gate, but I would need a lot of time and I was not sure whether the bars would be sunk into concrete below the ground. I wondered whether three days of constant work in the evening would get the job done.

The road outside the house and around the front porch was comprised of patches of asphalt, dirt, and mud, and across the street grew thick spiky bushes that I could not identify. If I ever got that far, I would have to steer clear of the bushes – they might be poisonous, or sprayed with poison to keep animals away.

A cold breeze blew as I made my way toward the other end of the property. I mounted the steps and stood on the rubber area, then inserted a rod into a hole and balanced on top of it, trying to see what was beyond the wall. A vast yellow desert lay before me, and I could spot tiny houses spread across the horizon.

I wobbled dangerously, and had to spread my arms for extra balance. If I fell forward, I would unquestionably die.

A canine of some sort darted across the desert about a thousand yards away, but I couldn't identify whether it was a dingo or a coyote. Above me, vultures swept the sky, their eyes trained on the ground, their huge wings blankets of death. They watched the canine, sweeping after it into the haze where I could no longer see them.

A loud scream from the house startled me, and I tumbled to the rubber, bumping my elbow. I scrambled up and twisted to look.

"Get out, pig," the man yelled. He was holding one helper by her hair and as I watched, shoved her out on the sand and rocks.

"Forgive me! I didn't mean to!" She scrambled onto her knees, clasping her hands at chest level and lowering her head.

"Family, come out! Everyone, come out," he yelled through the open sliding door. "You too, Gretta!"

I picked myself up carefully and began to creep down the steps, heart beating hard. He was focused on the girl, but I was terrified he would spot me and ask what I was doing on the wall.

He stood over the woman and leered down at her as I inched, step by painful step, back into the yard. His family joined him. I crept into the cover of the plants, gripping a coarse stalk, and watched the people assemble in a line, their hands clasped in front of them.

The man put his hands on his hips and looked at the line. "Disobedience and disrespect will not be tolerated in this house. Especially when it comes from the help." He turned to the helper, who shrank away and began to sob. "You have a shelter, you are being fed; I saved you from the labor camps. Do you want to go back?"

"Dad?" The younger child raised his hand and got a nod from his father to speak. "What did Molda do?"

"The ungrateful idiot brought me cold soup, and I generously asked her to reheat it instead of directly punishing her. Maybe it was a mistake to be kind. So what did she do? She threw the bowl and broke it – an expensive bowl, as well."

"Forgive me! I didn't mean to. I just – I just – I slipped, I was – it was o-one of those days when you f-feel you scarcely have control of yourself. I'm s-so sorry," Molda sobbed.

The man raised his hand and Molda covered her face, flinching. He grabbed her wrists and moved her hands, then slapped her several times.

"If you don't want to work, don't. I took you in because your brothers begged me to, but I will throw you out tomorrow if I want to. All you have to do is let me know you don't want to work." He paused, breathing hard. "And if you think of hurting any of us with something in the food, I will make sure they treat your brothers really well, until they die slow, painful deaths. Do you understand me, Molda?"

The girl nodded. Her worn dress was stained with sand and dust, and I could see tears in her eyes.

"Your punishment is to clean the entire area in front of this door. Plan for ten or twenty yards, and you can use the humanoid. I'm also punishing him; he is learning discipline. You should get along well together. Don't drag; you have two days to finish." He turned toward me and grinned. "Or else."

"Small human," I said to myself. I stared back at him until they all went inside.

CHAPTER 7

We each had a broom and we battled endlessly against the sand, which blew back in pretty, silvery drifts with every taunting puff of wind. I kept my distance from Molda, but I could see tears in her eyes whenever I glanced her way, and occasionally she sniffed.

I longed to strike up a conversation; Father had told us that a suffering human would be more compassionate toward us, and I wanted to know if it was true. I was also sorry for her, with smarting red cheeks and swollen eyes. The work was horrid; sand got in our faces and up our noses, and once or twice, I had to stop to cough the retched stuff from my throat, where it burned like shards of glass.

When I saw her watching me for the second time, I decided to try my luck.

I started closing the space between us, moving toward the pile of sand she had swept up. I took on the more laborious job of sweeping it away from the stretch we were clearing, leaving her free to sweep more into the cleared space – a slight gesture. She looked at me, holding her broom, and gave a half-smile and another sniff.

"Your hair looks nice," she said.

I felt my heartbeat pick up, but tried to stay casual. "Really? I didn't think so." I paused and looked at her, taking in her soft, walnut eyes and dark hair. "Your eyes are beautiful." I couldn't think of anything else to say for a moment. "You know… our eyes are smaller than yours."

"I know." She didn't seem to think it was a silly comment, but rather an invitation to look a little more closely at me. "Your hair is a bit – a bit like fur. I hope I don't offend you, but… but…" Another small smile brightened her face. "I wish I could stroke it – like a rabbit. I think you should look in a mirror and see what I mean." She giggled.

I looked at my hands. My hair had certainly grown, and I could barely see my knuckles or my knees, but that told me nothing about how my face looked.

"Keep sweeping; he might be watching us." She sighed. "What do you call yourself?"

I set my broom to work again. "We are small humans. Like you, but small. The same, but small." I spoke proudly, making it clear I would have no other name.

"I know what you are, silly. I mean, your name. You heard him spitting my name – Molda." She brushed harder, tucking her left leg behind her right one. "Pleasure to meet you."

"Snow."

"Snow what? Do you have a family name?"

"No. Just Snow. We are not that many, only a couple of hundred in our village. Small humans don't live long, so we won't run out of names. Instead, we use our year of birth, if we need to. I am Snow 2222."

"Oh. That's nice." She hesitated. "I would be Molda 2219."

I nodded, pleased that she was interested and respectful enough to try out our traditions on her own name. She looked at me for a second, then grinned a bit. Her eyes were still red and her cheeks redder, but she seemed comforted.

"Let me fetch a mirror and come back. You should see your face." She laid the broom down and moved toward the door. "Don't worry; I'll pretend I'm fetching some water."

More than a few years had passed since I had last looked in a mirror, and that had been before the freezing. When she returned, I took it tentatively and looked down at an unfamiliar face. I wasn't sure how to feel about it, but it was not what I had expected. It was not how I felt. I could see now why the man had likened us to monkeys.

"Wow. I don't know what to say. I thought my hair was long, but not this long. I look... I look like a lion."

She giggled again. "I like it, though it looks dense and rough, not like mine. Maybe our hair genetics are different too."

She was not being rude, merely curious. I could handle curiosity. I brushed away some more sand, suddenly becoming aware of how much my stomach ached from emptiness. We were not fed well at the best of times, and though "breakfast" was not a luxury we enjoyed, the thought of going until tomorrow evening, or even longer, without food...

I glanced up at my newfound ally. She was free to move

around the house as she wanted. She often worked in the kitchens.

"I've had no food since last night, Molda… if you were in the kitchen, could you… could you maybe swipe me a piece of bread?"

Molda looked alarmed and went back to sweeping, shaking her head.

"Please, no. I wouldn't even dare think of such a thing. Master Bunly will punish me severely, and I'm afraid he might hurt my brothers too…"

I nodded, disappointed. Bunly. So that was the man's name.

There was silence for a moment and then she looked at me again. "Do you know the camp near the Rocky Mountains?"

I stared at her for a few moments, wondering how *she* knew that camp. "Do I? We lived in the Rocky Mountains, near the top, before they raided our place. I know the camp, though it's not exactly near the mountains. A few of our elders and fighters used to visit the camp for medication, but they had to walk over four hours to reach the place."

She nodded. "My brothers work in that camp. They're all three older than me, and they knew I couldn't survive the harsh work, so they asked Master Bunly to take me on. Gretta gets most of the work done in the house, so Master Bunly employed me as a favor. The Master is one of the many owners of that camp."

She wiped her face. "And you know, he doesn't mind looking at young women – not that he does anything, but… he walks between the tents, checking out the working women. Gives me the shivers. Ugh." She blotted at her face again.

I was silent, deliberating. If she knew the camp and her brothers worked there, we might be nearer home than I'd thought.

"Listen, what is this place? Is it a town?"

"This is called the Grove – it's a sort of little settlement. All the previously habitable cities in the area were either poisoned during the war or became too dangerous to live in because of bandits. This place is under the control of the Marshals, so… at least we don't have to worry about that."

We kept sweeping, and I noticed the air cooling as the sun began to set.

"It's getting chilly, right?" I asked.

"Yes, in the evening the temperature drops twenty or thirty degrees. Sometimes hail falls, it gets that cold up there." She jerked a thumb at the clouds. "Whatever you do, never put one of them in your mouth if that happens. Treat it like rain. It's all sulfur and other toxins." She paused, then looked embarrassed. "Maybe you already know that."

I smiled and nodded.

"I like you, Snow. You're smart."

"I sure hope I am, but that's up to Monster Bunly." I shrugged.

"No, it's up to you too. Be obedient and let the time pass. Just say yes to whatever he asks. Avoid speaking to him unless it's absolutely necessary. He really hates being spoken to unless he's given permission." She glanced at me, face sympathetic. "He has a problem with humanoids."

"Ah. Please. Small humans," I interrupted.

"Small humans. You know, you aren't the first pair he's bought. I've been here about four years, and have seen five humano- small humans."

"What happened to them?" I looked up at her sharply.

"They died..." She looked away.

"How?" I bit my lip, feeling sick.

"He brought the first two and the last one alone. They all died of sickness at the doctors' unit, probably caused by the sun rays. The work on the wall is too strenuous, and... well, you don't need me to tell you the food isn't nutritious. In the middle, he got a pair, two brothers, but after they'd been here a little while, they got increasingly irritable and started refusing to work." She glanced at the house to check we weren't being observed.

"What happened?"

"They sat by the wall and refused to answer his calls to come inside to sleep. When Master Bunly wants to sleep, everyone has to turn in. So he marched toward them, but when he got near, they scrambled up the steps onto the wall and rolled two rods from the top, trying to hit him in the head. But the rods missed his head and landed on his shoulder. He screamed in pain and went pelting up the steps toward them. They jumped back down into the yard."

"And what happened?" I asked impatiently.

"Give me a chance to catch my breath. He ran back down, and they started hitting him with stones, and he got madder and madder. The smaller one bit him, and the other managed to get up onto his back and started hitting him on the head with a stone. It was horrible – we thought they'd kill him, no matter being small, but the Master gets crazy when he gets furious. He threw one across the yard and beat the other one so bad that the poor thing could barely breathe."

The brothers' story crushed my hopes of finding a way to throw the man off his legs or outwit him. I felt sick, but I had to hear it out, so I kept sweeping and let her talk.

"He went inside the house and we thought he would call the marshal, but he just ordered us to go to bed. You know how quiet it is here at night – you can hear every sound. I didn't want to listen, but we all know what happened."

She looked down at her brush, face tight. "We heard screams and grunts; we assume he finished them. I never heard the car, so I guess he buried them in the garden. Somewhere near the corner, I assume under some plants." She glanced that way, but I couldn't bear to look. It was all I could do to hold onto the broom and keep my feet.

"Murderer. Monster."

She was shivering from the cold, and I felt it as well, but I did not shiver. I was too shocked and too angry.

She looked at me. "Just... watch out. Don't let him hear you say anything foul about him. He is merciless. You've already bitten him once. Don't do it again."

I nodded. "I'll try. No point getting on his nasty side unless

I have a plan." My stomach growled its agreement, and I pulled a face, going back to my brush.

"Think well. Oh, and he likes it when you call him Master. Try that when you have something to ask." She wiped her hands, then shuddered again. "I will see you tomorrow. I have to go in; the weather is getting too cold for me. We'll finish tomorrow."

We looked at the vast expanse of half-swept sand, already blowing back into place, and then she wrapped her arms around herself, nodded at me, and went inside.

An hour later, the man – I would not call him 'Master' in my head – came out and told me to stop working. I put the broom down and took a step toward our room, but he stopped me, eyes cold.

"You'll be sleeping out tonight. I think you can feel how cold it's going to be, and maybe that will encourage you to appreciate the man that shelters you. Next time you get any clever ideas about biting me, I won't be so nice. Do you understand?"

I ground my teeth, drew a deep breath, and made myself say, "Yes, Master." It tasted bitter on my tongue.

CHAPTER 8

The evening passed slowly. I sat and watched the sun sink, tensing and relaxing my muscles as the ice crept into my bones. The temperature had dropped to a couple of degrees above the freezing point, and it was still light enough that I didn't dare start anything for fear of being spotted. Finally, the last of the light died away, and I dared to move from my hunched huddle on a stone.

I walked around the house and surveyed the area where I had finally decided to dig the tunnel. The place where the perimeter wall met the gate would be strategic for keeping a low profile, but would also prove hard to penetrate at the angle I wanted to try, so I started digging under a plant. If I was lucky, I would be able to conceal the hole, using the plant as a decoy. I tried not to think about what I might find if I had been so unfortunate as to choose the spot where the brothers were buried.

I dug all night, even to the point of shaking with exhaustion. The work kept me hot, and after what Molda had told me about the man, I was determined to win our freedom. I would not have him murder Caramel. I would not have him hurt her. We were not going to die of radiation or starvation, either. I occasionally paused for short breaks and hugged my arms to my chest, shivering and muttering to myself to keep moving.

By early morning, the hole was about two feet deep. I was so tired, I could hardly lift my arms, but I climbed carefully out of the hole, making sure I didn't dislodge any of the edges. I gathered up the loose sand and scarce soil and scattered it across the garden to hide what I had done, and then I went back to my rock from the previous evening and shivered with exhaustion and cold.

By sunrise, I felt very dizzy, and desperate for anything – bread, grass, even a few weeds. I eyed the plants around the garden, but I couldn't risk eating any. I didn't think I would be able to manage a full day's work on no food, especially when we were fed so little anyway. To take my mind off it, I got up to walk.

I paced back and forth in front of the sliding back door which he usually came through, and at every turn, I blew warm air on my hands. The digging had kept me hot, but now I was damp with sweat and freezing. My hair stuck uncomfortably to me, and I was increasingly aware that I had no clothing. The thought of walking naked in front of someone's sleeping quarters made me feel deeply ashamed.

The door slid open suddenly, and he stuck his head out.

"A bit cold, I see." He looked amused. "I'm glad you didn't freeze overnight; I want the worth of my coins, and I haven't had it yet."

I kept my head down, trying to stop shivering.

"Brrrr…" He mocked, "Do you have something to say? Mmm?"

"I am sorry, Master Bunly. I learned my lesson." I could have cried at that moment. I felt so humiliated, so defeated and small. I swallowed hard and looked up at him. "Master Bunly, please can I have a small piece of bread? I cannot work unless I eat; I will faint." I gripped my stomach as I spoke, hating how my own body betrayed me and gave him power over me.

"Bread?" His laughter hurt my ears. "I'll throw you a handful of yesterday's weeds. Only what your sister didn't finish."

He handed me the key to the room, and told me to eat what was left in the bowl, leaving me with a burning question: how did he know Caramel hadn't finished her dinner? He never came back after delivering our food.

I ran to the other side of the house, down the hallway, and to our room, panting. Thankfully, Caramel seemed unhurt; she was sitting on the floor, washing her face. When I asked, she said he had simply checked on her earlier and then handed me the bowl of leftover greens. I eyed her, sure she wouldn't tell me if he had hurt her – she would know I'd have to seek revenge, and would also know what might follow at the hands of that monster.

My stomach ached throughout the day, and my mouth dried up. My limbs shook with tiredness, and my hands were blistering from the digging. A few stems were not much to sustain me, and I longed for the evening, for the chance of fresh food, whatever it might be.

Caramel managed to finish the lens cleaning and check-up without complaining, and I noticed she worked hard at it, but by the time we were hammering the rods, the whining had started. I didn't blame her; she was younger and less capable physically, and the heat made her dizzy and sick. We had started earlier than usual, as I hoped we might be given food sooner if we finished, and feared I would pass out if we left it too late – but that meant working in the hottest part of the day.

As much as I could, I comforted her. I kissed her a hundred times and told her tales about our small human champions, which had often been told in our caves at home. I hoped that they might ignite a fighting spirit within her, because we were going to need it if we were going to survive.

"Here, Caramel. Sit in the shade here and rest a little in between helping me with the rods," I told her. "You must look like you're helping, but if you crouch like this, they shouldn't be able to see what you're doing from down there; you might be lifting the rods or checking on a lens. Take a break in between, and we'll be done before you know it."

I moved along the wall a little at a time, checking the holes wherever there was supposed to be a rod. In places, the rubber had melted and the hole had disappeared, so I had to look carefully for remnants of the red painted mark. At each, I erected a steel rod and hammered it down until half of it had disappeared.

The hammering was the most straightforward part; whether the steel rod clicked on the rod below or not, I had to remove it, either because a new rod wasn't needed, or because I needed to put a bismuth one in.

The problem lay in removing the steel rod. The man didn't own any tools for grabbing it, so to get it back out, I had to wriggle and twist it to loosen it within the hole. My hands were slippery with sweat and because it was so much hotter than when we usually worked, the steel rod soon became too hot to touch.

I couldn't remove the steel rod, so I started using bismuth on the next hole. I hammered down until the rod disappeared, and a sense of satisfaction brightened my day a bit. I had found a way to make the task a little easier. I could still feel if the rod needed replacing, so I didn't see the point in using the steel one and then taking it back out; it was just more work.

In the late afternoon, the man brought me a bowl of greens and told me that Molda would not help me clean the sand because she was busy inside the house. The news crushed my hopes of another discussion with her; I had wanted to gather as much insight as possible. Any scrap of information might make the difference between a successful escape and a failure.

I ate quickly, though it made my stomach cramps worse. The sudden shock of food was almost too much for me, and I had to sit for a little while before I could even hold the broom steady. As soon as I was able to, I got up and began sweeping, hoping to finish early so I could work on the tunnel while they had their dinner. My window might only be an hour.

Left and right, I swept as I hummed an old tune, keeping my feet moving and refusing to think about how much I ached and how the sand made my mouth gritty and sore. It would be worth it to be free, I reminded myself. It would be worth it not to have to see my sister brutalized. It would all be worth it, in the end.

The sliding door opened and the man came out, carrying two chairs. He invited his wife to take a seat. Both boys came out and stood behind their parents, waiting for instructions. I glanced at them warily, but kept sweeping until the man addressed me.

"I want you to exercise with the children. This is a form of training I conduct for them so they can strengthen their muscles and improve their reactions. Never know when they might need them."

I nodded, wary.

"Don't go to the end of the garden; stay here where we can see your moves. Run, and avoid letting them catch you." He cleared his throat. "Boys, your mission is to capture the humanoid. To give you a bit of an edge, use these sticks." He held out two thin, wicked-looking sticks, and I tensed.

"Aw, just like the marshals use!" the younger boy said.

"Yes, just like the marshals use. You can try to catch him with your hands, or trip him up, or you can try hitting him on the head with the stick."

"But Daddy, won't that hurt the boy?" The older child eyed me, and I felt a brief scrap of hope that at least he was concerned. Maybe humans *were* taught cruelty, rather than being inherently cruel.

The man scoffed. "This ain't a boy. He's an adult, but these freaks don't grow. You won't kill him. The sticks are only wood, not metal like the marshals' sticks, and they're hollow. Anyway, even if you kill him, you don't need to worry about it."

I took a deep breath and assessed quickly. The boys were almost double my size, so I would have to make use of every advantage and turn my slightness against them. I stepped back as they approached, one on each side. I wondered whether I should let them catch me quickly and get it over with – but instead, I decided I could have a small act of revenge.

The first boy swung at me, but I dodged; I could tell I was going to be faster than them, and that might be enough to keep me safe. He swung again, and the second one lashed out too. I darted back, quick on my feet, and dodged another swipe, then turned to run.

They pursued me across the hot sand, and I felt my feet skidding and skittering, but I kept ahead of them – though once or twice, I felt the air thud with motion as one of them swung. I ran around the house, and they both followed, keeping up with ease.

The older boy ran ahead, and suddenly I was trapped

against the corner of the house, near the entrance to the hall which led to our room. Caramel had gone inside, and I wished she was there to see what I was going to do. I hadn't planned on them cornering me exactly here, but I'd known they would catch up somewhere, and I had an idea.

The first one let out a roar as he charged at me and swung the stick overhead, leaving plenty of time for me to move. The stick slammed into the ground, and its vibration startled the boy, giving me a second of opportunity. I stepped forward and yanked the stick, knocking him to the ground.

Out of the corner of my eye, I saw the man stand up. I walked toward the other boy, giving him a chance to swing. He faked a swing from the left, but I held my ground for the feint, and then ducked the actual blow, throwing my hands down into the sand so I could drop without losing my balance.

"Very clever," the man said coldly as I picked myself up. "You're quicker than I expected. Let's see if we can re-balance this a bit." He brushed past me and went into the house, leaving the three of us panting and waiting. When he returned, he carried a length of rope. I balked and tried to step away, but he grabbed my arms, held my wrists together with one enormous hand, and then tied them tightly.

"Now," he said, his eyes hard. "How about we try that again?"

I looked down at my bound hands as the older boy regained his stick, and then I turned and ran.

The game was very different now. With my hands tied, it was a challenge to keep my balance; I tripped and staggered, and more than once, felt the bite of a stick on my head, shoulders, and back. My hair cushioned the blows, but they stung fiercely in places, and I was breathless and hot, desperate to escape. Behind me, I heard the younger boy squealing with delight at the game.

I ran ahead, glancing over my shoulder to see if I had gained any ground, and then my foot came down on a rock and I lost my balance. They overshot me as I fell onto my back and I got a moment's respite from the swings. As I sat up and spat sand from my mouth, it occurred to me that I had mostly been defending, and I could attack for once.

I stayed on the ground, chest heaving, and waited for the boys to turn back to me. As the younger of the two approached, I put my weight on my torso, brought my legs up, and delivered a powerful kick to the younger boy's knee. He screamed and dropped, and the man was suddenly towering over me.

"Stop," he ordered.

I picked myself up, panting, and dusted some of the sand and filth from my hair.

"Inside, boys," he growled. His wife moved from her seat as well, and the man stood beside me as I panted and trembled and watched them go in. When the door had closed, he looked down at me.

"Lesson number two. If you touch one of the boys again, I will kill you."

"Sorry, Master." I looked up at him. I could feel my muscles jumping with adrenaline and exhaustion. "...just excited."

He narrowed his eyes, then smirked. "I don't buy your crap.

You'll sleep outside again tonight."

"Master Bunly..." I swallowed hard. "Please, can you re-move the rope?"

He turned his back and left. I gritted my teeth as the sliding door closed with a thud and I was left alone.

CHAPTER 9

I missed Caramel badly. The departure of the sun was the departure of any last vestiges of warmth and I was left shivering and freezing as the sweat from the chase dried. My new bruises ached, and places where the sticks had grazed me stung.

I moved from corner to corner of the yard, assessing which was least exposed to the wind, but eventually I settled near the sliding door so I would know when they had gone to bed. As I crouched and shivered, I glared at the ropes on my wrists and thought.

Father's voice came to me, as I crouched miserably in the darkness. His words were small comfort – just musings on a centuries-long animosity – but it still helped me to hear them. "There is no shame in losing, especially if your opponent is much stronger than you. And you might think the tall humans are our enemies, but they are not. The ignorance of some tall humans is our enemy."

The man was ignorant, but I would not lose to him. Shame or no shame, I would protect Caramel at all costs.

Once I was sure they were asleep, I wrestled my hands free

of the rope and returned to my tunnel. I removed the decoy plant and dug with my bare hands, moving toward the gate until I hit the rod which fixed it to the ground. I dug lower until I found the base, only to discover that it was sunk into concrete as I had feared.

I sat in the hole and stared at the dirt for a while, trying not to let myself drown in the hopelessness that threatened whenever I looked at that impossibly hard grayness, with the iron rod buried through it. No amount of willpower would break it. No tool I could fashion would even mark it. It seemed impossible.

I rested for about half an hour, thinking. Low spirited, yes, but not beaten: my determination hadn't slipped an inch as a result of the concrete. When I had regained a little energy, I set to work digging to the side, pushed on by the drive to keep Caramel safe.

I dug almost fanatically. I was keenly aware of the freezing earth and the cloying dark, of how scratched and scraped and sore my hands were, but I carried on, hoping to find weak concrete or a short gate rod.

It was gloomy, but moonlight shining into the hole was enough to show me when I finally found it – a rod not rooted in the concrete. The concrete below it was cracked and worn, and soil seemed to have got into the mix, perhaps when they were laying it. The constant test of frigid nights and hot days flexing it, even deep underground, had helped, and there were cracks running throughout. With enough time on my hands, I could break through.

By the time I felt the sun's first warmth, I had cleared enough to have a fist-sized hole between the rod and the base. I went back to the house and apologized to the man, and he ordered me to start the work earlier than usual because Caramel would not join me. "I have another task for her," he said.

I went up onto the wall and began working on the lenses, waiting for the sun's rays to peak at noon. I felt so sick and dizzy that at points I had to sit down and lean my head against the stone's cool relief. I would have to rest soon, no matter the consequences – and yet, how could I?

Worry drove me blindly on, and I hardly knew what I was doing. I kept looking over my shoulder at the house, wondering what task he had in mind, and whether she was alright. What do you do against an oppressor? I could find no way to reason with such a cruel man, and I had no chance against him through brute force. All I could do was dig and hope for a miracle.

I looked over my shoulder again as I started on the rods, and finally glimpsed her burnished hair, bright in the sunshine. She was on a ladder, cleaning the facade of the house. She glanced back at me and cocked her head down, dropping her eyes.

I felt myself grow cold, despite the heat of the day. She looked so sad and exhausted, the distance of the yard removing any illusions about her thinness. She was worse than when we had arrived, and I was terrified she was getting sick. Being here was breaking my sweetheart.

I sat down for a moment, giddy. A thousand thoughts of what they might have done to her swam through my mind, until I had to grip the stones to know which way was up. I had to find a way forward. Could I poison him? Could I sneak to his room at night and stab him? Could I trip him and split his head on the rocks?

No. I had no access to the kitchens. He locked us in at night – or me out, at least recently. I had neither the height nor weight to trip him, and there was nowhere outdoors I could lay a trap. No, I had to be cleverer than that.

I forced myself to stand back up, and looked at the bismuth rod I was using in place of the steel one. It was still in the hole I'd hammered it into, but there was no need for it there, so I reached out and grabbed it, and found it was stuck fast.

My stomach twisted. If the man saw, I didn't know what he would say, and he was bound to see. While he kept out of the radiation himself on the whole, he checked on our work regularly, especially when we were dealing with the rods.

I grabbed the rod and tugged, then leaned all my weight on it and wrenched as hard as I could. It was slippery and my hands slid along the length, but it didn't budge an inch. I stared at it and then the sun's heat suddenly vanished from my back; I looked up to find the man standing over me, his face grim.

"Idiot. If I give you instructions, why don't you follow them? Eh? You think you are smarter than me, chimp, but you're damnably stupid." He pushed me aside and kicked the rod, freeing it with little effort. I grabbed it and tugged it from the hole.

"When you leave the bismuth for more than a few minutes, there is a high chance that it will mold to the rubber," he snapped. "Stupid. I don't have time to punish you now; I'm leaving on an errand. I'd leave you to shiver another night outside, but there's no cloud cover and you're so useless, you'd freeze. I've still not had my coin from you. Next time, use the damn steel." He clipped me, and strode off to the steps.

I rubbed my head, gripping the bismuth. How could any thinking entity, human or small human, be viewed so cheaply? With force and a few coins, you had power of life and death over a creature of equal awareness and thought. How had our world come to this?

Caramel finished her task and joined me at the wall, but insisted fiercely that nothing had happened in the house. When I pressed her, she said she was exhausted and feverish. I felt her forehead and drew my hand away; she was burning.

Even when we were back at the village, the elders hadn't spared medicine for Caramel's fevers; it was a precious resource, and had to be saved for infections. They knew she was strong enough to sweat through them, suffer though she might. If we could get them, protein-rich foods seemed to help, at least once the fever had cooled, but those were rare enough too. In these conditions, I didn't know how she would cope.

I sat her in the shade with some water and struggled on with the work myself. I think she fell asleep.

We went to our room to rest before the evening's work, and for the first time, Molda brought our food because the man was away. I asked her if she could bring us anything with protein for Caramel, but she said that although they had powdered protein, she couldn't bring us any because the man monitored the tub. She said he checked routinely because the powder was very expensive, and only the children should have it. It was kept in a low kitchen cupboard, she said, and she had never even opened the cupboard door.

I had hoped to talk to her more while we cleaned, but I had only just picked up the broom when we heard the car's engine, and the honk of a horn. A moment later, Gretta came out of the house and told me to go and help him.

He had already unloaded sheets of metal that looked like an unassembled cage. I held my tongue and waited for him to speak.

"We need to take this to your room. Follow the instructions to the word, if you're not too dumb. Carry. Walk. Unload at the door of the room." He turned and went into the house through the front door.

I moved the sheets around the side of the house, exchanging glances with Molda whenever I passed her. When I had finished, I knocked on the sliding door. He came out and went straight to the room, then opened the door and told Caramel to go and help Molda.

He took a piece of paper from his pocket and read through it quickly, then set it on the floor, and started putting the pieces together. Every few minutes, as he connected the hinges, he would tell me to hold on to the sides. The cage started forming, and I felt no doubt that we would sleep in it tonight.

The crumpled paper lay in front of my eyes, so I tried to read the title. "Por. Fact. For. Mi. D. Yom. Si. Ze. Ani. Mals."

The man looked up, glancing at me and then at the paper, and then began to roar with laughter. He dropped his screwdriver and banged his fist on the floor, howling. I stepped back, able to feel blood flooding to my face and tears in my eyes. I pressed my hands over them, and then yelped as he grabbed me by the waist. He lifted me up and I caught a glimpse of the corridor as he strode through the hall, still chuckling.

When we reached the sliding door, near where Molda and Caramel were sweeping, he opened it and yelled for his family, his voice still thick with laughter. He put me down and I stood, quivering with humiliation, as they arrived, already grinning. His tone must have tipped them off. Molda and Caramel kept sweeping, and I avoided looking at them.

"Read for us, monkey." He waved the paper at me.

I took the paper and cleared the lump in my throat. "Perfect for medium-sized animals." I didn't need to read the sentence; I already knew what it said.

He smacked me on the back of the head. "The second line."

"Roo. S. Ter. Rooster. C. Ca. Ge. Cage. G. goo. Good." I kept my eyes on the paper; the boys had begun to laugh too, and the wife was giggling. I swallowed, then risked a glance at Molda. She was not laughing, but staring at the ground she was sweeping. Caramel had stopped and buried her face in her hands. I felt so ashamed of my inability to make sense of the letters that were evidently so easy for my tormentors to read.

"Continue, please." His wife was smirking.

I sniffed, eyes burning, and forced myself to speak. I felt a tear streak down my face as I stumbled. "F. For. T. Tran. S. S por. Ta. Tion. Transportation."

The man howled again, shaking with laughter at my attempt.

"How can it be so stupid!" the elder boy chuckled, elbowing his brother.

"Look, he's crying! Crybaby!" the younger boy mocked.

I turned and started back around the house. I didn't care that I didn't have permission to go. I didn't care what he did. I didn't care if he shut me out. Death would be more merciful than ridicule.

He came back a while later and continued assembling the two cages. As he put the last hinge in place, he gave me a grin. "F. Fo. Fo… Fo… tansputtation, was it? Wonder what I bought these things for." He chuckled again. "Pity you're too dumb to read the paper."

I took a deep, slow breath and pretended I hadn't heard. "Master Bunly, are we supposed to sleep in the cages?"

"Yes. I don't want you to breed."

He was not a monster; he was an ignorant monster.

CHAPTER 10

Father used to say regrets define the man, and the decisions define the regrets. One should be wise when deciding on something related to one's fate, or the fate of another. Crying made me shameful but not regretful; the whole incident was not a choice.

When I woke the next day, I could see that Caramel was weaker. She had her eyes half-closed and had not moved from the sprawled position she slept in, though she was clearly awake.

I had to find a way to get her protein; when the fever passed, she would need good food to rebuild her strength. I wondered briefly if I could catch a bird, but I had never seen one in the yard, nor any other animal. The man had said the wall was electrified, which was probably why we stood on rubber when we worked on the lenses. I could probably jump from the top of a rod to the top of the wall, but it would do me no good if I got fried.

Caramel was lying diagonally in the cage to maximize the space for her legs. She tried to stretch her arms, but paused when her knuckles bumped a bar, and adjusted to stretch vertically. I was glad to see her move, at least, but the lethargy didn't leave her face.

"Morning." I sat up stiffly. "How are you feeling?"

"Morning." She paused, seeming to think for a while, and then sat up too and touched her head. "Not bad, not good… I don't know. I don't know anything. I want to go back to the life we had. This is a nightmare, Snow." Her lip quivered. "I'm not strong, like you. I can't – I can't take the heat, I c-can't take standing there, knowing about the radiation, knowing that we're going to die." Her voice rose in pitch, and I bit my lip, wishing I could reach over and comfort her.

"I know, honey. I am working on a way to escape," I said.

"But what if we get caught?"

"We have to not get caught. I'm not worried about the punishment, but if we get caught, we won't be able to use the tunnel again. The man will know about it."

"What if he doesn't punish you with sleeping out? What if he hurts you? Hurts you real bad?" She paused, rubbing her eyes, and then frowned. "What tunnel?"

"He won't kill us. He paid a lot of money for us, and he doesn't want to lose it. He wants us to work our asses until we drop dead." I clenched my fists. "No one can take the sun's rays at their peak for a year, Caramel. We are as good as dead if we don't escape. We have to try."

"What tunnel?" she whispered.

"When he made me stay out at night, I dug a hole next to the gate. I dug down to the base where the rods are welded to the foundations, and I found a section where it's weak. I started removing the concrete and now we have a hole, but it's not big enough yet. I need more time." I looked at her. "Today, while we're working, you keep an eye on the house, and I'll dig a bit. I'll come back, move a rod, and then dig a bit more – hopefully without anyone noticing."

She looked at me, eyes gleaming in the gloomy room. "I'm afraid, Snow. Leaving isn't easy... we don't know where we are. If we don't die of starvation, we'll die from the sun's rays. There's no shelter out there. And even if we manage to survive both, how will we know if we've entered a radiation zone? How will we ever find anywhere we can be safe?"

I drew a deep breath. I had thought about all those things plenty of times, but I still came to the same conclusions. We had to leave. "Then what do you suggest we do? Be slaves for a year and wait for our deaths?"

She shook her head sharply, then whimpered and pressed a hand to it. My heart ached for her.

"No, not wait until we die, but wait a little longer than this. We might... we need to find a sure way to run away."

"There is no sure way. What do you expect? That we could just steal the car that we don't know how to operate and drive away? I wouldn't even be able to reach the peddles. What magical answer can there be to these problems? We just have to risk it."

She opened her mouth, and then we heard the slam of a door, and we both fell silent.

The heat increased throughout the day, and I was convinced it was the hottest day since we'd arrived. The work seemed torturous. At times, I thought my heart was going to burst through my chest, as I darted up and down the steps, working on the rods and finding moments in which I could dash down on the pretext of getting a drink or fetching something, and slip into my hole to dig. Every time, I checked the plant was still in place, but I feared the decoy would fall if there was a strong wind or if the sand under it slipped.

By afternoon, the hole under the gate was big enough that my head could fit through, but my shoulders were still too wide. I scrabbled experimentally at the soil on the other side and found it was more compact, probably from the regular footfall, or the weight of vehicles.

Caramel did much of my work on the rods, but before the sun was setting, I found her sitting in the shade, faint and white. I hoped our meal would revive her, but she had no appetite. Her fever had passed and she needed to eat, but I couldn't persuade her to do any more than promise to try later.

I left her in the room and went to help Molda with the sweeping. It appeared the man had forgotten his own deadline, but we kept it up, just in case it was some trick or game of his.

I was no longer in the mood to chat with her, but she seemed to sense my misery and kept tossing me smiles whenever our eyes met. It was hard to ignore her; she seemed to instinctively know how to lighten the mood.

"The Master's taking a nap right now. If you listen well, you can hear him snoring," she said cheerfully, after making sure we were unobserved and far enough from the house that we couldn't be heard. "It's so loud."

"Really? I can't hear a thing. Where is the room?"

"Up. To your left."

It would be directly above the hallway on the right side of the house.

"I can't hear anything."

"Listen well. It sounds like breathing from down here, but when you're near the room, it sounds like an engine." She signaled me to shush and pointed at her ear.

I cocked my head to one side and concentrated. "Oh. That's him? Wow."

"Yes. He eats a lot at lunch and almost always takes a nap directly after. Sometimes it's only for twenty minutes, but he's always got to sleep a bit. He's been asleep hours today." She giggled. "It'll be suppertime before he wakes up!"

I looked down at my broom, then glanced toward the room where Caramel was resting. "... Listen, since he's sleeping... You said the protein powder's in the white bucket in the cabinet next to the stove, right?"

"Yes, it – wait. What are you thinking?" She eyed me. "Don't be a fool. If anyone sees you, you won't like it at all. You'll sleep in the cold again, or worse!"

"I don't care." I shrugged. Another night in the cold would be unpleasant, but it would let me finish digging the tunnel, and I didn't feel as though I had any other choice. "I have to. Caramel is getting weaker and weaker. Back home, when she could rest, she could just sleep it off, but now... She won't be able to fight the illness without protein." I didn't add that if we were going to run, Caramel would need at least some reserves of strength.

Molda stared at me. "What illness?"

"Nevermind."

I put the broom down and made my way to the sliding door. I opened it slowly and peeked inside, able to feel my heart starting to beat faster. There didn't seem to be anyone around. I paused for a moment, orientating myself and working out the best route to the kitchen, and then I crept in.

It was the first time I had been inside the main house save my disastrous excursion with the man, and I felt terribly small. The furniture dwarfed me, the windows seemed miles above my head, my feet vanished in the plush carpet… but Caramel needed me, and I pushed on. I was glad I had a good memory; I knew exactly where to look for the kitchen after last time.

I could just reach the kitchen door handle, and I let myself in quietly. There was a square of cloth on one of the counters, perhaps used for drying up, which I managed to snag by one corner. It would do as a makeshift bag.

I opened both cabinets by the stove and found the bucket. I knelt on the corner of the cupboard and pulled it toward me, then cautiously eased the bucket open. To my horror, it made a popping noise that startled me so much I almost dropped the cloth. I froze for a few seconds, then scooped up two handfuls of the powder and bundled it into the cloth.

The house seemed quiet and still, so I got up, clutching the cloth, and hurried out of the kitchen to the hallway. I thought I was safe, and then, like an apparition, the older boy was suddenly standing to my left. I glanced at him, then started hurrying toward the sliding door, hiding the cloth in front of my body. I prayed he couldn't see it. There was a moment of sickening silence aside from the padding of my feet in the carpet and then –

"Hey, stop!" he cried. "Thief! Daddy!"

I wrenched the door open and ran past Molda, still clutching her broom. I knew I would only have minutes, so I wasted no time on her "what have you done?" and rushed on to the room we slept in. Caramel was lying down, but sat up when I entered.

"Quickly," I said, thrusting the cloth into her hands. "Protein."

"Snow -"

"Eat it."

She sprinkled some of it on her tongue, staring at me doubtfully.

"Caramel, quickly," I urged.

"It's dry! It makes me cough, I -"

I pushed the bowl of water to her and watched as she forced as much of the powder into her mouth as she could and mixed it with a gulp from the bowl. It made her gag, but she shook the last of the dust onto her tongue, and washed it down again.

I could hear loud footsteps. "Hide the cloth beneath you. Fast!"

The man appeared at the door, his eyes heavy and his expression dark as he stared at me.

"Monkey. What have you done? Did you steal something?"

He put his hands on his hips.

"No, Master Bunly. I am sorry, I made a mistake." I didn't know what else to say. Anything might give away that Caramel had been involved, and I couldn't bear the thought.

"What did you do, you little devil?" he growled. He was so tall. I squared my shoulders and drew a deep breath.

"Nothing. I got thirsty and wanted to fetch myself some water. So I–"

He grabbed my hair and yanked me outside.

"Liar. Liar!"

He slapped me in the face a couple of times, and the slaps stung badly, making the sky reel and dip over my head. He was so strong, I couldn't shake his hands off, and when he dropped me, I staggered onto my backside.

He went inside, but not for long enough for me to gather my senses: he was back in what seemed an instant, carrying a rope. I felt sick and tried to turn away, but he merely grabbed me and knotted the rope around my neck, then yanked me to the door frame and tied the rope high up on a nail there.

"Molda, go inside. And you, devil, will sleep here tonight."

Alone, I tested the knots. I thought with my hands free, I could loosen them, but he had pulled them too tight, and my tiny fingers could not undo what his huge hands had done. I tugged fruitlessly, sniffing with frustration, and then tried to sit to give myself a moment of rest.

The rope was too short – there was little slack when I was

standing, and I couldn't even crouch without strangling myself. Within an hour, my legs were shaking and I could not stand any longer. I burst into tears and began to bang on the door, desperate for any relief. It was a long time before the monster came.

"Master Bunly, Master Bunly, I can't breathe," I sobbed, scrabbling at the rope. "Pl-please, *please* take it off. I beg you, Master. I can't sleep standing up. By sunrise, I will be dead for sure."

The man took one step outside, and for the first time I caught a glimpse of exhaustion on his face. He reached above my head, released the rope from the frame, and went back inside without a word.

CHAPTER 11

T he cold did not bother me too much that night. I spent most of the time in the tunnel once I had calmed down. Within a couple of hours, I had removed the concrete soil mixture. The task was not an easy one; I broke a fingernail, and the sharp end of the bar pierced my skin, causing a well of blood that looked blacker than the darkness of the tunnel, and stung horribly.

However, the pain was nothing to the joy I felt once I had scraped away enough soil to crawl to the other side of the bars. There was still a lot of hard ground ahead of me, but my success gave me energy, and I struggled on until I had surfaced on the other side of the gate. From there, I checked that the house was still and quiet, and then I drew a deep breath and ran to the next gates.

I thought I would pass out with joy. I fitted through these bars with ease; there was no need to dig another tunnel, which might so much more quickly have been detected. I slid through both gates, and then stood on the street and drew a long, slow breath. The air tasted different now. It had the spice and vivacity of freedom.

I walked a few feet along the road, looking for anywhere we could hide. On one side of the house, a metal fence lined the side of the road, and behind it, the endless desert. On the other side, the thick spiky bushes stretched skywards, impenetrable. It was not encouraging, but I was too buoyed by success to care; we were almost free. I sat down to wait for dawn to bring more light.

As soon as the sky began to brighten, I drew a deep, long breath and then ran to the end of the road, feeling light despite the night's work. And my hopefulness was rewarded – some luck at last to break through the overwhelming run of horrors: a fenced garden with the gates left open. We could slip inside and hide.

I looked back the way I'd come and decided I should return before there was any chance of me being missed by the man. It was a longer walk than I had thought, but eventually, I was standing by the house again, panting a little.

The visible hole in the front garden near the vehicle could be a problem, and a plant decoy wouldn't do the trick out here where there were no other plants. I looked around for something to cover it with in case the man had cause to go out today.

The surface around the porch was broken in many places, covered in rubble and cracked tarmac. I managed to find a strip of peeled-off asphalt wide enough to cover the hole, and pulled it into place once I'd crawled back inside. I just hoped that it looked convincing from above, and no one would step on it.

It was hard to go back, but I would rather have died at his hands than left without Caramel. I delivered a mumbled apology to the man and then got on with the chores for the day. In spite of another night spent awake and the exhaustion of digging, the work seemed easier, the materials lighter. I waited until we were up on the wall to tell Caramel, rather than risk being overheard while down in the yard or in the house.

The news didn't excite her as much as I had expected. She gave me a doubtful look, fingering a bismuth rod. "Snow… the road… we might be seen. What about whoever owns the garden at the end? What if they catch us? What will we do once night comes? We might walk hours only to find no more shelter, and then we'll die of radiation."

I pushed the last rod into place, and wiped my face, able to hear the man yelling at us to finish. She set off down the steps without further conversation, so I followed her and we went indoors for a break and a drink.

"Good thing we have nothing to pack," I said when we were alone.

She nodded slowly, then looked up at me. "Snow, the tunnel is there, so let's wait for a week and see what happens."

I stared at her. "Are you crazy? We're as good as dead if we stay here. Nothing else is going to save us – what's the point in waiting?"

"Maybe if the marshals came…"

I scoffed. "Even if the marshals came for something, they wouldn't do anything. Purchasing small humans is legal, remember?"

She wiped her eyes. "I know, but I'm frightened that someone worse than Bunly could catch us. We don't know what they might do to us. At least if we wait... well, we don't know what might happen. He might have a change of heart. Or he might drop dead."

I shook my head sharply. "Or he might *not,* and they might find the tunnel. We can't just accept a miserable fate because we aren't sure that the future will be better. We have to try, and if we get someone worse, then we'll run away again. I'll look after you."

A minute passed and she did not respond.

"So, in the early evening before he locks us in, and while they're having dinner, we will leave."

"But it's dark. We won't find our way."

"I already walked down the road and found a place where we can hide until morning. Running away in the dark is better; he won't run after us. We can hide in the shadows, and we're so small – even if he follows, he'll never find us."

She nodded.

After resting for a little while, I joined Molda in cleaning. The front space was looking much clearer, and even if we hadn't been planning to leave, I doubted whether we'd have much opportunity to speak again. I was silent as we started work, wondering whether I should tell her, or whether that would be a mistake – possibly a fatal one. I thought of her brothers in the camp, and of how she had been kind to me without reason, and I chose to speak.

She stared at me for a while, holding her broom, and then smiled. "I said you were clever, Snow. I knew you were. I'm so happy for you both."

"Do you know any nearby place we can run to? Any place

that comes to mind?"

"No. I've never been outside the house here except to ride in the car, and even that only happens once in a blue moon." She was silent for a few seconds and then said, "but I know a place you should go to."

"Where?"

"I've heard about a coalition formed between humans and small humans, a little settlement just north of Los Aconos."

I studied her for a moment. "I have heard of Los Aconos, but never of the coalition. I thought that settlement was nearly empty. Some of the elders went there once, many years ago."

"It's news I heard about a year ago. Now and then, there's a story about an attack on a small factory to free small humans, or an attack on caves to free human prisoners. Gretta and I talk about it sometimes, once the family have gone to bed. We both think the coalition must be behind the attacks, though of course, we've no way to be sure."

I stood very still, heart singing with hope. Peace between races, a place that would protect us, a place that fought and took risks for the rights of others. The blank fear that loomed on the edge of my success's elation felt suddenly less overwhelming.

"Thank you, Molda." I nodded hard. "How do I get there? How do I move from here?"

She looked sad. "No clue. You can walk, but you'll have to stay away from the roads and avoid the sun at its peak. If the moon is full, you can walk all night long, but you'll need to carry enough food and water. I traveled by road once with my brothers, before all… this. I don't remember much, but I know you can't go two days without finding new food and a water source."

There was a shout from inside the house, and she put her broom down quickly, then looked at me. I hadn't said exactly when we would run, but I think she had understood this would probably be our last meeting – and we would scarcely even say goodbye. "Be careful out there, Snow," she said, and then turned and hurried inside.

CHAPTER 12

I stared at the beautiful violet sky, resting my chin on the broom. The sun was nowhere to be seen, and in less than one hour, the light would disappear. Father had told us that sunsets only became violet when the radiation began; before that, they were pinks and golds and oranges. I stared up at the deep purple. How could something so beautiful be so harmful?

The door slid open and Molda was back. She stepped out with two chairs, cleared her throat, avoided eye contact with me, and turned and went back in. Within a minute, she returned with another couple of chairs.

She glanced inside and quickly whispered to me, "Guests."

I nodded and drew a deep breath, pretending to be calm. Strangers. Human strangers. My stomach did a backflip.

Gretta and Molda set up dishes and cutlery on a small table between the chairs, and I stood resting my back on the wall near the hallway, wondering whether I might just disappear to the room.

Bunly, his wife, and two guests came out and sat at the table. One was an old fat man who had lost all his hair, except for small patches on the temples. He looked like a balloon with fur stuck on. If I had stretched my arms wide, I could not have covered his belly. The other guest was a woman with gray hair and big eyes. Her face was heavily lined with care.

'... cost me a pretty coin or two,' Bunly was saying to the man, gesturing at me. I gripped the broom tighter.

Gretta and Molda brought out two serving plates, piled high with food. I moved a step closer, spotting steaming baked potatoes atop a bed of glistening rice. I swallowed heavily at the mouth-watering sight. The scent of herbs and fresh garlic wafted from the plates as they were set down, and I had to look away. When had we last eaten anything that would do more than keep us alive? We had not even had our night's weeds yet.

'Take him and feed him, Molda. I don't need him drooling all over the place,' the monster growled. 'Humanoid, go to your room and eat.'

I stared at him for a second, then turned to go indoors, stomach in knots. I had not counted on them eating outdoors, but I went silently, not wanting to draw more attention to myself than was necessary.

As I walked back to the room, I thought frantically. There would likely be very little time between them finishing and the man locking us in. We could run tomorrow morning, but he would likely follow, unless we risked the radiation and fled when the rays were at their peak – and even then, I had seen his radiation gear. I didn't know what to do.

Within a few minutes, Molda came to us with our food

plate and I picked up my head, able to smell instantly than it was more than just thistly greens and chewy stems for once. Rice. Our food had a handful of amber rice on top, soft and tender-looking. I glanced at Molda, wide-eyed.

"Something extra for the road. Finish eating quickly because he wants you to go back out."

I felt my stomach clench. "Why? Did he say?"

"No, but before the sun sets." She left. I picked up the bowl, and drew Caramel to my side so we could savor the real food. No matter what was coming, it felt good to put something with substance in my stomach, and the taste – it was indescribable, soft and buttery and salty and sweet all at once.

"Humanoids! Come outside!" We had barely finished eating when Bunly's shouts echoed down the hallway.

Caramel grimaced and stood up. She took my hand, and we walked together. I felt like we were two sheep, heading for the final act in a slaughterhouse.

"Do as he says. Don't disrespect him or disobey him while the guests are there," she whispered.

I nodded. For the first time, I wondered if my behavior troubled Caramel more than what Bunly did.

The man's sons had joined the group outside, standing near the table, which was littered with the remnants of the meal. I eyed them nervously, remembering our last encounter. The man had evidently not forgotten it, either, for he turned to his guest, grinning.

"David, the white one is so fast and feisty. He bites, he scratches. He thinks, that one. But my boys are smart and strong too. Imagine, there might be a ten year difference between them, and the boys could still beat the freak!"

The bald stranger grinned. 'Ha! Can't wait to see it! I like a bit of spitfire!'

The woman rolled her eyes and shook her head.

"Boys, take your positions on the left. Humanoid, come."

I approached him.

"Do I have to tie you? If you so much as take a swing at one of my boys, I will break your arm. If you trip one of them, I will break a leg. If you bite, I will pull out your teeth. Understood?"

"Yes, Master."

I knew I had to throw the fight away. Once we finished this charade, I would be leaving the place with my sister for good – if not tonight, then soon. We would walk to the garden in the evening; the next day we would make our way toward the high rise buildings. Gangs and bandits might control the buildings, but we might also find the coalition. Anything, even death, had to be better than this.

The boys yelled, pummeling their chests with their fists, waving their sticks, and then charged as a unit. I took off to the side, darting away from them, and then changed direction and ran back toward the table. They tore after me, and I could feel the ground bumping beneath their weight. I swerved and tried to dodge, but one managed to hook my ankle with his stick, and I staggered and fell into the sand.

A rain of blows came down on my back, and I heard cheers, felt spit. I clenched my teeth and pressed my face into the sand, focusing on thoughts of our escape. The sticks hurt, but weren't heavy enough to injure. Put up with the humiliation a little longer, just a little longer, and we would be free.

I could hear cheering and laughter, and then the scrape of a chair and the monster's voice. "Good, boys, good. I think that's enough for tonight – it's getting dark. You'd better be heading in to bed."

"What a show!" The bald man laughed.

Caramel's small hand appeared in my vision, and she helped me up, looking shocked and tearful. I gave her fingers a quick squeeze to show her I was alright, and then turned to look at the monster and his guests. He gave me a big, smug smirk.

"Well done, humanoid, you are learning," he said. The other man clapped him on the shoulder, and they turned to go in with the others, while Molda and Gretta started clearing the table. I signaled to Caramel to move.

We strolled away from the table and the helpers, moving casually until we were no longer visible. If Molda noticed, she gave no indication. When I was sure we wouldn't be seen, I put on a spurt of speed and ran to the hole I had so carefully dug, and moved the plant. Caramel joined me more slowly, staring at it.

"Get in. Come on."

She froze, her dark eyes fixed on the hole.

"Don't be afraid, come on," I said.

She didn't move a muscle; she closed her eyes, and a streak of silver raced down one cheek. I swallowed hard. I hated to see her cry.

"Okay, I'll go first and you follow me, but put back the plant."

She nodded, and I climbed down into the hole, breathing in the smell of the damp sand. I crawled to the gate and squeezed through the gap I'd made.

"When you get here, feel the bar; you have to go below it."

I gave her a few seconds to assess, then climbed further and pushed aside the asphalt cover so I could clamber out into the front garden and make room for her in the hole. I lay flat on my stomach and stuck my head down the tunnel.

"Where are you? Pass your head and shoulders through first and then push your body. I fit, so you will."

"Here."

I lifted my head, and there she was, still on the other side of the gate, her eyes black as bullets and very wide.

"Snow… Snow, please, please, come back inside, let us do it tomorrow at noon." Her words were very quick, and she sounded breathless. "The darkness is frightening. My heart is going to stop. Please. Please, tomorrow, tomorrow, Snow, I promise we'll try t-tomorrow."

I froze, able to see a shadow on her side of the wall, suddenly visible as someone approached in the last of the dying light. I shut my eyes for a second, praying desperately that it was Molda.

"Come quickly," I breathed, forcing myself to open my eyes.

"Where are you? Humanoids? Come!" Gretta's voice sank my heart, and I had no clue what to do except wait. I could see her now as she rounded the corner, and then stared at Caramel as she strode over.

'Caramel,' I hissed, drawing into the shadows of the gate. Caramel didn't move; I could see her trembling, and before she could drop into the hole, Gretta had her by the arm.

"Where is your brother? What is this!" She stared around for a second, and then drew a deep breath.

"Master Bunly! The humanoids are escaping! Come quickly!" she screamed.

I leaped up from my stomach and ran.

CHAPTER 13

No one was in the garden, and I found a cool, comfortable spot under one of the trees where I could regain my breath. I was shaking from the dash through the final two gates and the race up the road, but so far as I knew, nobody had seen or pursued me. I was alone in the stillness of the garden, surrounded by cool blues and peace.

I was so tired, I thought I might fall asleep, but no sleep came. Whenever I shut my eyes, all I could see was the monster towering above Caramel, hurting her, tearing her apart – and it was all my fault. I had no choice but to go back, to try and save her, even if it meant I died. She was my sister, and there was no one to protect her but me.

I spent some time whittling at a stick with a stone, sharpening the end to a point. I imagined attacking the man from behind when he came out of the house to get in the car. I stared at the weapon, feeling sick. Father had taught us that most of the miseries brought on by humans were driven by greed, and that weapons were the device for this greed.

Even with the sickness, I longed for a gun. The simplest solution would be to shoot the man dead.

Attacking him from behind might be ineffective. I recalled what Molda had said about the fate of the small human brothers who had attacked him at the wall. However, I was determined to try. Before I had escaped, I was saving myself and my sister from tyranny and injustice. Now, I had to save her from the punishment she would face for my behavior.

A car crept along the street beyond the garden, headlights dipped. It was very late for a vehicle to be out and it moved slowly; I suspected the man was searching for me. If he caught me, I doubted I would survive his wrath. I shrank more deeply into the bushes, breathing slowly, and waited.

Once the sun had risen, I slipped out onto the street, staying low near the bushes. I made my way back down the street, and found a small hollow where I could slip into the cover of the spiky bushes there. The task was much harder than I expected, and the bushes scratched me no matter how careful I was. I pushed aside thoughts of them being poisonous – there was no point thinking about it now. The ruby blood dried in my white hair, dark crusts marring its purity.

I waited for hours, and he did not come out of the house. Time passed achingly slowly, and I wanted to scream with despair. Instead, I shifted my feet and waited more. At any moment now, Caramel should start working on the lenses, and she would be able to hear me if I shouted for her.

Finally, when lunch had passed and Bunly ought to – I hoped – be asleep, I built up the courage to creep across the street, through the gates, and go behind the car to check the hole. As I had feared, the hole was filled, and the whole area around the gate had been sprinkled with white powder. It had to be poison. I stared in despair at the undoing of all my work, at the clear attempt to kill me, and then slipped back to the bushes to try and think clearly about my next step.

If I had a chance to stab him in the neck with the stick, I would kill him. If I could strike his head with a rock a few times, I might knock him out. There were more rocks here, ones I could lift which might do enough damage. I stayed crouched among the bushes and kept sharpening the stick, wishing I had thought to prepare a second one.

Suddenly, Caramel walked past the gate, staggering with the weight of a rod. I sat up very straight, heart pounding with relief – she was alive. "Caramel!" I hissed. She didn't hear me; no surprise across that distance. I leaned forward in the bushes. "Caramel!"

She walked on, stumbling with the rod. I bit my lip, watching as she had to sit down to rest. "Caramel!"

She got up again and moved on, getting further away from me. I waited, breathing hard, and watched as she had to sit again, several times. The rod was far too heavy for her.

An idea struck me as I watched her struggle onto the wall. Once more, I left the haven of the bushes and slipped towards the gate. As she drew close to it on her way back, I hissed her name again. She looked up, her mouth opening with surprise, then turned her eyes back to the floor and approached.

"Snow... I am so sorry."

"Don't be. We'll figure this out. Just don't be afraid. Do you promise me not to be afraid?" I leaned into the gate, cursing the bars that separated us.

She nodded.

I so badly wanted to ask if she was okay, but I held my tongue. I waited a few seconds, staring at her, and then spoke again. "We were so close."

She covered her face with her hands and I bit my lip.

"No, don't, I didn't mean to put you down, honey." I drew a deep breath. "It's not your fault. I should have made you go first. Running away is scary, and it's okay to be afraid. Listen to me."

She looked up, eyes bright in the sun. I leaned closer. "We were so close, and we can do it again."

"Tell me what to do."

"I'll lie down on the floor near the gate, and you go fetch Bunly. Tell him I was injured and I can't move. Say you saw me crawling, and then I went still – you think I'm dying. As soon as he comes out of the gate, I'll leap up and hit him on the head."

"What if he catches you? What if *he* hits you on the head?" she whispered.

"Then I'll run away. We have to try."

"He will lock the gates. It won't work, Snow!"

"It will work because he has the keys on him. You said you would try. What else can we do? The hole is filled, the ground covered with poison. Even if we had the time to dig another tunnel..." I gestured all around me at the white stuff. "I don't know what it is, but I daren't dig through it, or leave you alone that long."

She nodded, wetting her lips, and I drew a deep breath.

"Check that he is alone and outside the house; we want him to come on impulse. And come with him, stay close. If I don't see you behind him, I'll run away. No point in getting him to unlock the gate if you aren't here."

She nodded, eyes wide and glassy with fear. "I love you, Snow."

"I love you too, baby girl."

I lay down on the ground behind the car, placing my left hand on my stomach. I planned to tell him I had been poisoned by the bushes. I counted the seconds, my heart racing.

The stick and the rock lay near my right hand, concealed by my thigh. I imagined him grabbing me up from the ground, his fist closing on my hair, and me whipping the stick from nowhere and stabbing him in the neck.

I heard the crunch of footsteps, and peered sideways through my lashes.

"Hello, idiot. You will be punished."

"Mercy. Mercy, Master," I mumbled, and faked a cough.

I heard the clatter of his keys and the squeal as the gate opened, and then I saw him. He shut and locked the gate. Behind it, the glimmer of brown hair – Caramel.

"Mercy. Forgive me, Master."

"Mercy?! I will teach you a lesson you won't forget," he growled. I could feel how hard he was stamping as he moved toward me.

"Ohhh, forgive me. Now I know what it means to have shelter and mercy. Please, Master," I muttered.

My heart was beating so fast it felt like it was humming, and my breath caught in my throat – snagging as though I had never learned to breathe properly. Lying still took every iota of self control I had; I wanted nothing so much as to leap up and run. I could feel myself trembling.

I peered up at him, and he had never seemed so tall before. Lying on my back, he looked like a giant built of pure power and malice, and I'd never been so scared in my life.

"I will break your fingers to teach you a lesson for stealing the protein, and from now on, you will always be tied."

He stooped to grab me. I lifted my upper body, jerking backwards, and with a powerful swing, stabbed him with the stick. I had imagined it driving into his neck, but I was far off and only hit his lower thigh.

He screamed, almost deafening me. "Devil! I will kill you!" he roared.

I leaped away, feeling giddy. I no longer knew which way was up, barely even knew what the present moment was – everything honed in on that single idea: kill or be killed. I gripped the stick and stabbed him in the thigh again.

He screeched and dropped to one knee, but I was too shocked and slow to dodge, and in another second, he had me by my throat. Panicked, I set the butt of the stick against my hand and stabbed at him over and over again. Once, twice, three times, until I saw the blood spurting from his stomach, and he dropped me.

I knelt and grabbed the rock, and struck him on the head

several times. He went limp against the hot ground. I took my stick up again; the sharp tip had only stained about half an inch. The wounds were not fatal, and I had to get Caramel out.

The keys had already fallen from his pocket and lay next to him on the ground. I grabbed them and sprinted the short distance to the gate, my heart pounding. It was a challenge to get the first key into the lock; my hands were shaking too much.

Caramel stood there, looking as shocked and fearful as I felt. She put a hand through the gate and touched mine. The feel of her small fingers steadied me slightly, giving me a grounding in a world that was still spinning like a top.

The key wouldn't turn. I looked in her eyes and took a deep breath. The second key did not fit either.

Stiff with dread, I tried the third – and this one clicked.

"Is he dead?" she whispered as she crept through the gate to me.

"No, he is breathing. All the wounds are shallow."

I wondered if I should drive the stick into his throat and finish him. I owed it to other small humans – the dead, the others he would purchase in the future – and yet, did I want to be a killer when I was not under threat of death myself?

"Let us leave," I said.

Caramel moved giddily through the last two gates and down the road, but we made swift progress, driven by the heat of the sun and the blinding fear of what might follow. When we reached the garden, I felt I could breathe for the first time since last night, but then I looked back along the road to Bunly's house, and couldn't go further.

I knew. I had a chance, maybe the only chance that many small humans would have against such a criminal. He would buy more of us. He would treat them worse. They would not have the opportunity to dig holes and free themselves. There would be many more Snows and Caramels atop that wall, and I could prevent it.

Despite her protests, I left my precious Caramel in the garden, and began to walk back to where the monster was lying. If he was still unconscious, I would kill him. If he had woken up and entered the house, I could not. That would be my decider. I gripped my stick tightly, deciding that I was taking an active part in fighting for the cause. Maybe it would become my story for the coalition. At least, if nothing else, I would know that I had tried.

I walked down the road, and once I spotted his body still lying in the dust, I ran. I reached him, panting, and placed the sharpened stick against the soft part of his throat, below his Adam's apple.

"Bunly," I called softly.

I pressed the stick against his skin, denting the flesh. I wanted to look him in the eye, but without risk of him subduing me.

"Bunly."

"Mm," he muttered, and his body twitched.

"Bunly. Open your eyes."

The bulge in his neck moved up and down as he swallowed. He opened his eyes a crack, and then wide.

"We are small humans."

I shoved the stick with all my strength, driving it an inch into his neck, and then kicked it through.

AFTERWORD

Thanks again for reading the book, appreciating your time. If you enjoyed it, I would be immensely grateful if you could rate it and post a short review.

www.Jaykerk.com check my latest work, subscribe for giveaways, and check my social media.

A Predator And A Psychopath: A Dark And Twisted Psychological Thriller

"The character at the heart of the novel is both terrifying and realistic. For fans of dark thrillers and crime fiction, this novel will not disappoint." Self-Publishing Review ★★★★1/2

"Brilliantly narrated, a cunningly plotted novel that immerses the reader in a twisted mind and the complicated world of psychiatric medicine. I loved every bit of it." Readers' Favorite Book ★★★★★

Trigger warning: caution is advised, the book contains graphic content. Do not read this if you are at all weak-stomached or easily sickened / offended. Reader discretion is advised.

After Jason is committed to a mental institution, he begins to uncover things he never knew before or things his mind shut out to protect him. He finds himself questioning what's real and what's not. What happened to his wife, Lisa? Where is Lea? Why can't he remember what happened?

Meanwhile, Jerry is dangerous and unpredictable. He envisions a world where boundaries are broken down and he is free to enforce his narcissistic belief that he has a divine mission.

An explosive ending that is anything but expected, forgive yourself for shuddering throughout and after you close the book.

Drawing inspiration from real cases, and with well-researched, realistic characters, this thriller is not for the soft-hearted.

Readers speaking about A Predator and A Psychopath:
"A must read thriller that will have your head spinning. I'd definitely read another by this author, his imagination is wild, impressive, and addictive." Amazon reviewer ✫✫✫✫✫

"It is a very intense book that will raise your curiosity." Goodreads reviewer ✫✫✫✫✫

"Every now and again you stumble upon a rare find in a novel. And I'm happy to say that I've found that diamond in the rough." The Sexy Nerd 'Revue' ✫✫✫✫✫

www.ingramcontent.com/pod-product-compliance
Lightning Source LLC
Chambersburg PA
CBHW031312130726
47988CB00007B/2808